MY FIRST LOOK AT SEASONS

MAPLE TREES IN BRIGHT FALL COLORS

Fall

JILL KALZ

CREATIVE EDUCATION

Published by Creative Education

123 South Broad Street, Mankato, Minnesota 56001

Creative Education is an imprint of The Creative Company

Designed by Rita Marshall

Photographs by Corbis (James L. Amos), Dennis Frates, Tom Stack & Associates (J. Lotter

Gurling, Victoria Hurst, Thomas Kitchin, NASA/TSADO, Spencer Swanger)

Cover illustration © 1996 Roberto Innocenti

Copyright © 2006 Creative Education

Printed in the United States of America

Library of Congress Cataloging-in-Publication Data

Kalz, Jill. Fall / by Jill Kalz.

p. cm. — (My first look at seasons)

ISBN 1-58341-362-6

1. Autumn—Juvenile literature. I. Title.

QB637.7.K35 2004   508.2—dc22   2004056163

First edition 9 8 7 6 5 4 3 2 1

Fall

Not Hot, Not Cold

September is here! Birds fly south. Leaves change color. Kids go back to school. In the northern half of the world, September 22 is the first day of fall.

Fall is one of Earth's four **seasons**. The other seasons are spring, summer, and winter. Each season lasts about three months. Fall comes between summer and winter. Fall is also called "autumn."

COLORED LEAVES COVER THE GROUND IN FALL

It usually rains a lot in fall. It may even snow! The air feels cooler each morning. And the sun sets earlier each night.

Fall is a stormy time. Most hurricanes happen in September. Hurricanes are windy storms that spin across the oceans.

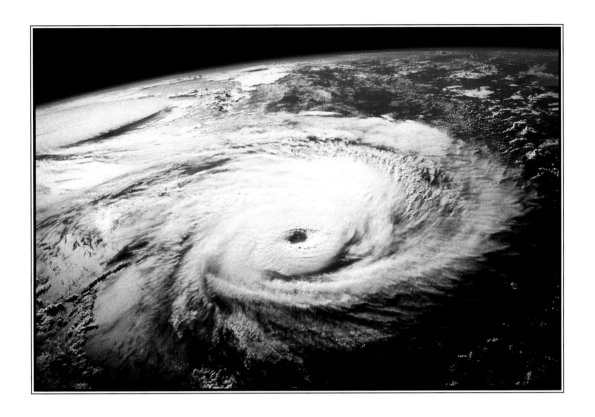

Hurricanes have names
just like people.
Andrew was one of the
worst hurricanes ever.

Getting Ready for Winter

In fall, many plants and insects die. This means that many birds have nothing to eat, so they must **migrate**. Geese, ducks, and other birds fly south to find food.

Some insects migrate, too. They cannot live in the cold. Each fall, monarch butterflies fly to California and Mexico to stay warm.

Earthworms migrate, too.

But instead of going south,

they go deep underground.

GEESE FLY SOUTH BEFORE WINTER SETS IN

Some animals start to **hibernate** in fall. Bats and snakes hibernate. They eat a lot of food. Then they find a safe place to rest.

Squirrels do not migrate or hibernate. They gather nuts in fall and store them in trees. They will need this food when winter comes. Food can be hard to find in winter.

On the first day of fall,

day and night are each

12 hours long.

SQUIRRELS SEARCH FOR EXTRA FOOD IN FALL

Colorful Trees

Trees make food in their leaves. When trees are making food, their leaves look green. Trees need a lot of sunlight and warmth to make food.

In fall, the days are shorter and colder. Trees stop making food, and the green color in their leaves goes away. Some leaves turn orange. Others turn red or yellow. Some leaves turn brown.

MANY LEAVES TURN BRIGHT RED IN FALL

Not all tree leaves change color in fall. Evergreen trees stay green all year. Pine trees and firs are evergreens. Their leaves look like green needles.

A Busy Season

Fall is a busy time for farmers. They **harvest** corn, beans, and other vegetables. They also harvest apples, pumpkins, and other fruits.

Big machines and tractors
harvest most of the
vegetables people eat.

FARMERS PICK UP BALES OF HAY IN FALL

October 31 is Halloween. Many people dress up like witches or ghosts on Halloween. Some kids go trick-or-treating. They ring doorbells and ask for candy. Thanksgiving is another special day in fall. Most families eat a turkey dinner on Thanksgiving.

Fall is a busy season. Enjoy it! Jump into a pile of leaves! Watch geese fly across the sky! Bite into a big, red apple! And then, get ready for winter!

PUMPKINS ARE USED AS HALLOWEEN DECORATIONS

Hands-on: Leaf Rubbing

You can look at fall leaves all year by making colorful leaf rubbings.

What You Need

Leaves of all shapes and sizes
White paper
Crayons

What You Do

1. Place the leaves on a smooth, hard surface. Make sure the veins (the raised lines on the leaves) are facing up.
2. Cover the leaves with a sheet of white paper.
3. Take off the crayon wrappers.
4. Turn the crayons on their side and gently rub across the paper. Use as many colors as you like to make a beautiful picture.

LEAVES MAKE COLORFUL PATTERNS WHEN THEY FALL

Index

Words to Know

harvest—gather food from fields or trees

hibernate—go into a very deep sleep for weeks or months

migrate—move from one place to another, usually to find warmth or food

seasons—the four parts of a year: spring, summer, fall, and winter

Read More

Buscaglia, Leo. *The Fall of Freddie the Leaf*. New York: Henry Holt & Co., 2002.

Hall, Zoe. *It's Pumpkin Time!* New York: Scholastic, 1999.

Maestro, Betsy C. *Why Do Leaves Change Color?* New York: HarperCollins Children's Books, 1994.

Explore the Web

DLTK's Autumn Activities for Children http://www.dltk-kids.com/crafts/fall

HalloweenKids.com http://www.halloweenkids.com

Kids Domain: Fall Fun http://www.kidsdomain.com/holiday/fall